JOURNEY
OF THE
WOLF

JOURNEY
OF THE
WOLF
The Beginning

Camilla Wolfe

Journey of the Wolf
Copyright ©2023 Camilla Wolfe. All rights reserved

Bare Bones Publications
Cover design: Book Designs by Shae
Typeset by: Shae Coon, GM Katz and Jessica Hughes

All rights to the work within are reserved to the author and publisher. No part of this publication may be reproduced, stored in a retrieval system, or transmitted in any form or by any means, electronic, mechanical, photocopying, recording, scanning, or otherwise, except as permitted under Section 107 or 108 of the 1976 International Copyright Act, without prior written permission except in the brief quotations embodied in the critical articles and reviews. Please contact either the Publisher or Author to gain permission.

This book is meant as a reference guide. All characters, organizations, and events portrayed in this novel are either products of the author's imagination or are used fictitiously. All brands, quotes, and cited work respectfully belong to the original rights holders and bear no affiliation to the authors or publisher.

Contents

Prologue 1

1 5

2 11

3 16

4 20

5 29

6 33

7 38

PROLOGUE

Long ago, when the world was plush and green, void of destruction and decay, the creatures of this world lived, created by the gods to inhabit and work the land they created. As time went by, the gods noticed an extraordinary creature. This beast would join with others of its kind and hunt, travel, and protect all in one group for the betterment of the pack. The gods were impressed by their love and dedication for one another and decided to give these creatures a name and reward them with the honor of being the protectors and leaders of their world.

The strongest of the pack was called to the foot of the steepest mountain and was given his orders. He would rule this land, and his family would follow in his footsteps after him. The gods named them wolves for their loyalty and friendship.

Decades passed with the gods in heaven and the wolves on the land watching, guarding, and sometimes... fighting. Other creatures grew restless and would attempt to cause harm to their world, but the faithful wolves were there to stop any foe to their world. Once again, the leader of the wolves was summoned to the foot of the mountain and given another gift. The gift of transformation. This gift allowed the wolves to transform from their wolfen state to one mimicking the gods themself. They would stand on two legs, their fur gone, and they would have the ability to speak in the god's tongue.

Peace fell over the land once more. Generations of royal wolves were born and led the different packs. One particular soldier wolf named Zeeb grew in status and soon became the personal guard to Princess Lupa. After years of service to the princess, Zeeb and Lupa fell in love, and through that love, the princess became pregnant. The pair were overjoyed, and to celebrate the happy news, Zeeb made his love a necklace in the shape of a crescent moon made from a rare moonstone that fell to earth long ago.

But not everyone was happy, for when the king discovered Lupa and Zeeb's hidden love and the child it created, he banished his daughter to a far-off land where she could have the child in secrecy and then return to marry a mate hand-picked by her father. At the same time, Zeeb was shamed and stripped of his duties to the royal family.

Lupa wept every night, and knowing the fate that awaited her child, she had the midwife promise that she would take her child away and keep her safe until she or the child's father could come and get her. But on the day of the birth, Lupa became ill and died soon after having her daughter.

Before she passed, Lupa gave her infant daughter the necklace given to her by her true love and named her daughter Luna.

Zeeb searched for Lupa for months and vowed never to stop searching for his true love. Until one cloudy morning, the king announced that the kingdom's beloved princess had died.

At the news of Lupa's death, Zeeb's once red beating heart became black with rage and cold as ice. With no more love for the royal family, Zeeb gathered an army and attacked the royal den one night.

The king of the wolves fought beside his pack. The battle lasted for days, but while his men died by the dozens, Zeeb was strong and could get inside the minds of his pack. An ability like the gods have never seen before. They called them the Army of the Dark.

In the end, the king reigned victorious. The gods were enraged by Zeeb's betrayal. They labeled the Dark army as traitors and demanded their deaths, but being the loyal wolf king he was, the king asked for mercy and that, instead, they be banished from Paradise forever. The gods agreed, but not before cursing the traitors, declaring them demons, and punishing Zeeb for his betrayal. He was drained of his blood until he was close to death and then cast down with the others to the pits of Tartarus, where he would eventually reign as king of a kingdom of darkness.

Knowing that the Dark Wolf's blood was full of evil and menace, the gods cast his blood from their earth and imprisoned it inside the moon. The white glow of the moon turned crimson and was named the Blood Moon. The land fell quiet as the wolves grieved their losses, and the red moon shone for one night.

Life went on as the moon regained its white luminosity. Little did the gods know, Zeeb made a promise before he was cast down.

CAMILLA WOLFE

A promise that he would come back and take over the land when the Blood Moon returned.

I

"Slow down, child! You are too fast for me."

"No, you're just too slow, Yaya!" Luna laughed but slowed her pace, so her grandmother could catch up.

Her grandmother came to her side, huffing and puffing. "You will be the absolute death of me, my moon," she says with a smile and pride in her eyes.

"Come on, Yaya, you are the strongest wolf I know. I have seen you go against some of the biggest alphas in the pack," Luna beamed at her grandmother.

"We are always stronger in wolf form, Luna, you know this, but" her grandmother stretches her back from side to side and groans when it clicks and pops. "it takes a toll on the human body. I'm afraid I'm not as strong as you once remembered, and one day, my body will be one with the earth again."

"Don't talk like that, Yaya. It makes me sad," Luna pouted, and her grandmother chucked her chin in playful reprimand.

"Do not pout, my child. Death is a fact of life, and we must all return to the earth. We must help keep the grass green, the trees growing, and the flowers blooming." She tips Luna's chin up to lock eyes with her granddaughter. "There is nothing sad about that."

"Can we talk about something else?" Luna mumbled, and after a moment, her grandmother agreed. They headed back to their home, hidden in the trees.

Luna sat at the window seat and read her books as Yaya tidied the kitchen after dinner. Her mind was filled with dragons and warrior princesses when she heard her grandmother coughing and gasping in the other room. Luna jumped from her seat and raced to her grandmother just as she collapsed. "Yaya? Yaya, wake up!" Luna shook her grandmother, but her eyes remained closed, her breathing shallow. "Hold on, Yaya, I'll get help." Luna left her grandmother, grabbed her phone from the window seat, and dialed 911.

"911, what's your emergency?"

"My…my grandmother won't wake up," Luna sobbed. "Please…please help me."

"Okay, honey. I need you to calm down and tell me what happened," the operator instructs Luna, and Luna tells her everything. When she was done, the operator instructed Luna to wait for the ambulance and make sure she kept breathing.

It seemed like forever before the ambulance showed up, and the EMTs loaded her grandmother in it before her grandmother was whisked away to the hospital. Luna is instructed to sit in the waiting room with a woman from child services who asks her questions about her grandmother and if Luna has any other family.

Luna shook her head. "No. She's all I have left," Luna choked and wiped at her eyes.

The woman looked at her with kind but sad eyes. "I understand. I lost my parents very early in my life. My uncle took me in, and I felt like I was completely alone in this world when he passed when I was twelve." Luna nodded in response. "But you know what?"

"What?" Luna asks.

"I soon found out I wasn't alone after all, and that there were other children like me that lost their families too. I lived with them in one big house until a wonderful couple adopted me." She made it sound so wonderful, but Luna was not convinced. She didn't want to live in a big house with a bunch of other children. She wanted to be with her Yaya in their little house in the forest — where she didn't have to hide what she really was. Where her wolf could come out and play amongst the other animals of the forest, human children would never accept what she really was, and Luna had yet to learn to control her wolf from coming out when she was angry. That's why Yaya had homeschooled her. Just thinking about the children staring at her with horror in their eyes made Luna shiver.

"For Iris Rella?" The handsome nurse taking care of her grandmother announced from the double doors.

Luna stood from her spot. "I'm her granddaughter." He smiled down at Luna before he ushered her through the doors, where a funny smell that had Luna cringing wafted up her nose.

She follows the nurse to a large door with her grandmother's name written on a small slip of paper beside the number 316. "She's weak but awake and asking for you. Go on in, sweetheart."

"Thank you," Luna mumbled and opened the heavy door to her grandmother's hospital room with a feeling of dread tightening her tummy. Luna couldn't stop the tears of relief that sprang to her eyes and trailed down her cheeks when her grandmother came into view.

"Oh, my child, don't cry. Come here, dear." Her grandmother smiled widely, and Luna didn't hesitate. She runs over to her grandmother and leaps into her open arms.

"I thought I would never see you again," Luna sobbed into her grandmother's chest.

"Oh, my dear, you will always see me again. Even if it is in the next life."

Luna pulled away and angrily wiped at her tears. "Stop saying that. I don't want you to die."

"Luna, that is not for you to decide. Only the gods can make that decision." Luna shook her head in denial but knew what her grandmother said was true. "Luna, I am afraid I do not have long..."

"Please, Yaya, don't...don't leave me," Luna cried and shook beside her grandmother's bed. As Luna's body trembled, her heart began to race, and her fingernails grew to sharp points as the wolf started to take over.

"Luna, child, I need you to calm down. Remember what I taught you." Her grandmother's voice was tender, and soon, it soothed the wolf that wanted to break free. "There you go. Calm, deep breaths." Luna took another deep breath as her heart slowed to a steady pace, and her wolf went quiet again. "That's my girl. You're getting stronger every day."

"I don't feel strong," Luna murmured, and her grandmother tipped Luna's chin up to look her in the eyes.

"You are stronger than you realize, my child. You have your mother's blood inside you, Luna, and she was the strongest wolf I know. Powerful beyond imagination.

And you," her grandmother tapped the tip of Luna's nose. "Are no different."

Luna smiled with pride. "Will you tell me about her again?" Luna loved hearing about her mother and how she loved her even before laying her eyes on Luna, how her mother was the most beautiful woman in the world with blonde-white hair, crystal blue eyes, and lips the shade of a summer rose.

"No, my child," her grandmother says, shocking Luna. Her grandmother never hesitated to talk about her mother before, and it hurt Luna that she refused now.

"Wh...why?"

Her grandmother sighed and gestured for Luna to pull up a chair. Once Luna was seated beside her grandmother's bed, she said, "Everything I told you about your mother is true. Her beauty, her kindness, her love for your father. But there is much more to your mother's story. I wanted to wait until you were a bit older, but it seems the time has come." Luna stares in confusion at her grandmother as she removes the necklace from her neck. The necklace her grandmother *never* took off. She holds the necklace out for Luna to take, and with a trembling hand, Luna grasps the warm metal in her hand. She always loved her grandmother's necklace, the silver crescent moon with the tiny red stone always glittering brightly even in the dark as though magical.

"This was your mother's, and now it is yours, Luna."

Luna gasps and clutches the pendant to her chest. "My mother's?"

"Yes. I was to protect it until it was time to pass it on to you. Until it was time to tell you the story of who you really are."

"What do you mean? Who am I?" Luna asks with trepidation, but her grandmother simply smiles at her.

"You, my child, are a princess."

2

Luna's heart raced with anticipation as her grandmother's words hung in the air. A princess? The thought seemed too grand, too impossible to comprehend. Yet, deep down, Luna felt a flicker of something - a connection to a world beyond her own, a destiny waiting to be fulfilled.

"What are you talking about, Yaya?" Luna laughed, but her grandmother lay stoic. Serious.

"Your real name is Luna Diamadis, and you are the last of your family. The last of the Diamadis royal line."

Luna jumped from her chair and shook her head in disbelief. "No, that's not true! It can't be true. I… I'm just a girl from Lost Sierra. I can't be a… a princess."

"But you are my child. Sit and let me tell you the real story of your mother."

Luna's head spun like a tilt-awhirl with everything her grandmother had just told her. Luna leaned closer to her grandmother, eager to hear the tale that would unlock the secrets of her true identity. The room seemed to grow still as her grandmother began her story.

"Long ago, there existed a kingdom ruled by a wise and benevolent king and queen," her grandmother began, her voice carrying a hint of nostalgia. "This kingdom was home to many magical creatures, including powerful werewolves like us."

Luna's eyes widened in awe. She had always known she possessed a special connection to nature, but to be part of a lineage of powerful werewolves was beyond her wildest dreams.

"Your mother, Princess Lupa, was born into this world," her grandmother continued. "She possessed an extraordinary gift - the ability to shape-shift into any creature she desired. This rare ability made her a beacon of hope and a symbol of unity among the different magical beings."

Luna listened intently, her imagination painting vivid images of her mother's adventures in her mind. She longed to be just like her, to embrace her true heritage and fulfill her destiny.

"But the peace was threatened by dark forces," her grandmother continued, her voice growing somber. "They sought to claim the kingdom's power for themselves and unleashed chaos and destruction, causing fear and despair to spread throughout the land."

Luna's heart clenched at the thought of such darkness tainting her mother's world. She could feel her own determination growing stronger, fueled by a desire to protect her newfound lineage.

"The king rallied the magical beings," her grandmother said, her eyes shining with pride. "Together, they formed an alliance of warriors, each with their own unique abilities. They fought relentlessly against the Dark Wolves forces, determined to preserve the harmony of their home."

As Luna absorbed the weight of her mother's legacy, she felt a surge of power and purpose coursing through her veins.

Her grandmother continued, her voice tinged with sorrow. "Your mother fought valiantly to bring you into this world, and in the end, she knew that only one of you could survive... and she chose you, Luna."

Luna's chest ached as she absorbed her grandmother's words. "My mother was a princess, and my father was, what, the devil?" Luna didn't know why that thought made her so angry, but the wolf inside her howled, and her eyes glowed red.

"Yes, but understand, Luna, your father was not always bad. He loved your mother dearly. I saw it myself, but times were different then, and your mother was meant to be wed to another royal."

"So, my grandfather punished my parents for loving each other?" Luna's voice turned to a husky growl, and her teeth grew to sharp points.

"Luna, calm yourself!" Her grandmother's voice was stern. So stern that it pulled Luna from her anger and allowed the wolf to sleep. "Luna, you have a difficult journey ahead of you. You must learn to control your wolf."

"What do you mean? What journey," Luna asked.

"The journey to find the *lefkí petra*, the White Moonstone. You must find this stone and take it to your family castle ruins, and there you must fuse it with the crimson moonstone *before* the next Blood Moon rises and the demons are released from Tartarus.

"What happens if they are released?" Luna asked hesitantly.

"They will rage a war that will end this world as we know it." Her grandmother answered with a quiver in her voice, and Luna shivered in fear.

"When is the next Blood Moon?"

"That I do not know. Upon my last breath, a guardian will arrive to take you to your ancestor's wolf den located in what is now San Diego. You will know this person by the moon and stone insignia on their uniform. You will train for your journey and find the answers you seek. You must not tell any human of who or what you are." Her grandmother placed her hand on the necklace. "Let your mother guide you, Luna," her grandmother said with a glistening tear on her cheek before her hand went limp, and she released her final breath.

Luna sobbed into her grandmother's bed while her wolf howled in grief when her grandmother's hospital door opened, and in walked a woman with ebony hair with tips the color of snow pulled into a tight ponytail, eyes as green as the leaves in her forest home and tall as a pine. Luna could see the woman was strong under the all-black outfit. Her face was emotionless as she watched Luna cry at her grandmother's bedside.

Luna stood, angry that this person would come into her Yaya's room uninvited. "Who are you? What do you want?" Luna knew she was being rude, but she couldn't help it. Her heart was broken.

Luna's eyes widened in shock as the woman straightened her back like a soldier, placed one arm behind her back and the other over her stomach, and bowed at the waist. "My apologies for disturbing you, Princess. My name is Sapphire. I am your guardian, and I have come from the Diamadis den. I am to bring you back." Sapphire said with a stern but not harsh tone.

Luna looked back at her grandmother, and more tears fell. "I don't want to go. I don't want to leave her alone."

"She is not alone, child. She has joined her pack in Paradise, and now it is time for you to come home to yours." Luna looked back at the tall woman, knowing that what the woman said was true. Still, her heart ached at the thought of leaving her grandmother.

"What will happen to Yaya?" Luna sniffled.

"The council members will take her back to her homeland to rejoin the Earth." With another sniffle, Luna nodded.

With one last kiss on her grandmother's cheek, she followed her guardian out of the room and into the cool fall air, where she would journey to her new life.

3

The ride to her so-called ancestor's wolf den was long and full of smog-filled air, concrete, and buildings higher than the tallest tree in Luna's and Yaya's forest. Luna hated it already. The city was a stark contrast to the lush, vibrant world she grew up in. But as much as Luna resisted, there was no denying that her destiny awaited her within the den's walls.

"I know this is all very strange to you, Luna, but you have a family here," Sapphire said, her voice filled with sincerity.

"They are not my family," Luna grumbled, her words barely audible.

Sapphire's eyes softened, filled with empathy. "Perhaps not by blood, but by loyalty to your mother. And there are children here around your age," she added, a glimmer of hope in her voice.

Luna's spirits lifted a little at the thought of companions her age. Wolves, just like her. Maybe this den wouldn't be so bad after all.

"And they're all..." Luna trailed off, curiosity tingling in her throat.

"Wolves," Sapphire confirmed with a nod. "All of them are training to become royal soldiers, just like you will."

Luna's eyes widened. She had always imagined being a princess would involve more ball gowns and royal events, not training to fight. "I thought I was a princess?" she questioned, turning her gaze to Sapphire.

Sapphire smiled softly. "You are, Luna. But being a princess doesn't exempt you from the battles that lie ahead. We must all be prepared to fight. I'm afraid the Blood Moon will call upon us sooner than we think."

Luna's brows furrowed. "And no one knows when the next Blood Moon will be?"

Sapphire shook her head. "No one knows for sure. Our mystics have consulted the crystals, but they do not give a clear picture. That is why we must remain vigilant."

As they approached the den, Luna's heart quickened its pace. The large iron gates loomed before them, adorned with the emblem of a half-moon, mirroring the pendant Luna wore around her neck. As the gates opened with a low whine, sealing her fate within, Luna couldn't help but feel a mixture of trepidation and excitement.

"Welcome to Diamadis den, Princess," Sapphire greeted warmly.

When her sneakers hit the pavement, four kids around her age came running out of the building, all dressed similarly to Sapphire. They stood in a straight line, their serious expressions betraying their youthful faces.

Sapphire gestured for Luna to follow her, and with hesitant steps, Luna approached the group. There were three boys and one girl, each possessing unique features. But it was the boy at the end of the line that caught Luna's attention. His untamed hair and piercing grey eyes held a sense of wisdom far beyond his years.

"These will be your guards and training partners during your time in the den," Sapphire introduced, touching the shoulder of each child. "This is Aria," she said, then continued down the line to each boy. "This is Marius, Galic, and this" — she touches the shoulder of the boy with the grey eyes— "is our most experienced soldier, Hunter. He is a descendant of one of the families that guarded your mother and grandparents."

As Hunter's gaze met Luna's, a swarm of butterflies took flight in her stomach. His presence was both intimidating and comforting, and Luna couldn't deny the connection she felt with him.

"It's an honor to meet you, Your Majesty," Hunter said, his tone respectful.

Luna felt her cheeks flush, and she averted her eyes, suddenly feeling self-conscious. "Can everyone just call me Luna?" she asked, looking up at Sapphire.

Sapphire's smile widened. "This is your pack, Luna. They will address you as you wish. However, in the presence of other packs, they must refer to you as Princess or Your Majesty."

Luna nodded, absorbing the information. Being called a princess would take some getting used to, but oddly, she felt a sense of normalcy among the other wolves.

"How long will I be here?" Luna asked, her eyes widening as they entered a grand hall, vast and filled with anticipation.

People meandered around the open space but stopped whatever they were doing when Luna's group stepped back, and Luna was left front and center. Then, like a fairytale dream, they all bowed.

"Welcome, Your Majesty," they all said in unison, and Luna's heart dropped to her stomach, and sweat lined her brow at the attention.

"Uh...Thank you?" It comes out as a question, but her fumble seems ignored as everyone returns to whatever they are doing.

Sapphire's voice held a note of uncertainty. "I cannot say for sure, Luna. We do not know the exact date of the Blood Moon's return. But I believe I can speak for the entire pack when I say that we hope you will stay and lead our family, just as your mother was meant to do."

Luna swallowed hard, feeling the weight of responsibility settle upon her shoulders. "No pressure," she murmured, a tinge of nervousness coloring her tone.

Sapphire chuckled, her laughter sending a wave of reassurance through Luna. "Come, Luna. Let's eat, and then Hunter will show you around."

Luna stole a glance at Hunter, her heart fluttering like a trapped bird. His grey eyes met hers, and for a fleeting moment, Luna could swear she saw a spark of understanding. With a nervous smile, she nodded. "Sounds good."

As Luna followed her pack into the dining area, she couldn't help but feel a sense of adventure settling within her. The path ahead was uncertain, but with her pack by her side, Luna knew she was ready to embrace her destiny and face the unknown with courage.

4

FIVE YEARS LATER

Luna's fist struck Hunter's ribs with a fierce determination, eliciting a grunt of pain from him. But he didn't falter. Instead, he retaliated with a lightning-fast sidekick to Luna's hip, causing her muscles to tighten with the impact. Their bodies moved fluidly, in perfect synchrony, as though engaged in a dance rather than a battle for supremacy.

"Getting slow, Princess? Too tired?" Hunter taunted, his voice laced with mischief.

With a quick feint jab, she caught Hunter off guard, landing a swift uppercut that sent his head snapping back. He staggered backward, a surprised expression crossing his face.

Luna, fists still raised, couldn't help but mock him. "Does that answer your question, soldier?" she taunted back, her voice dripping with confidence. She bounced from foot to foot, ready for whatever Hunter threw at her next.

Hunter, wiping away the sting from Luna's hit, couldn't help but flash a boyish smile. "After five years of training, it's about time you finally got a hit in," he remarked, his own confidence shining through.

Rolling her eyes, Luna removed the wraps from her hands. "Spare me your 'I am the greatest fighter since the ancients' speech again," she retorted, her tone laced with sarcasm.

Hunter shrugged casually. "Nothing wrong with telling the truth," he replied, bundling their wraps to toss them into the laundry basket. He then handed Luna a bottle of water, which she eagerly gulped down in three large swallows.

Luna gasped heavily, "There is when you won't shut up about it."

"Don't be jealous, Princess. You will get there one day," Hunter needles, and Luna rolls her eyes again at Hunter's ego. "On second thought...maybe not."

Luna's water bottle hits Hunter square on the forehead, only making him break into a fit of laughter.

Luna couldn't help but burst into laughter. "Would you shut up?" she scolded teasingly.

Their laughter was interrupted by Sapphire's authoritative voice calling out from across the training room. "Princess," Luna rolled her eyes at the formal address.

"Saved by the bell." Hunter smiled teasingly, but their smiles dropped at the concern evident on Sapphire's usually stoic face.

"What's wrong?" Luna asked, her voice betraying her calm exterior as she hurried over to Sapphire's side, with Hunter following closely behind.

Sapphire's gaze bore into Luna's, her expression grave. "The council has reported some unusual activity," she began, her tone serious. "Vegetation is dying off in vast amounts, and there was an unregistered earthquake in central Texas. Scientists are unable to explain these occurrences."

Predictably, Hunter chimed in, his voice hard as steel. "Let me guess, they can't figure it out, but we can."

Sapphire nodded, her eyes flickering with a mix of concern. "Indeed. And I'm sure you both have felt something off in the past few days."

Luna nodded in confirmation. She had been restless, unable to shake the feeling that something was amiss. That's why she had been training more fiercely with her guards, desperate to release the excess energy coursing through her like liquid lightning.

"It's the Dark Wolf, isn't it? He's preparing," Hunter surmised, his words causing Luna's inner wolf to snarl in response.

Sapphire confirmed his suspicion, her voice filled with a grim resolve. "Yes. He's spreading his poison upon the human world. While we can't do much about the earthquakes, our mystics are working discreetly to help the humans replenish their crops."

Relieved that action was being taken, Luna affirmed, "Good. I don't want the humans to panic. So, what are our next steps?" She looked at Sapphire, her loyal guard, for guidance.

Sapphire's gaze hardened her following words, carrying a weight of destiny. "It is time, Princess. You must journey to find and unite the ancient crystals before the Blood Moon."

Confusion furrowed Luna's brow. "But we don't know when the next Blood Moon will be."

A small smile tugged at Sapphire's lips as she handed Luna a tattered scroll carefully wrapped in a shimmering gold ribbon. "We do now," she said cryptically.

Luna unraveled the scroll, revealing the ancient script and symbols she had come to recognize through her studies. Her eyes widened in trepidation as she looked back at Sapphire. "Halloween? That's only a month away! How are we supposed to find two ancient crystals that even our best archaeologists and mystics couldn't locate in years? And all within a month?"

Sapphire's pride shone through her voice as she responded, "Not 'we,' Princess. You. Your guards will accompany you, of course, but you, Luna, are the one who will guide the way."

"Me? How? I don't…"

"The crystals are a part of you, Luna, and they will only call to you. That is why we could not find them ourselves. We have been waiting for you."

"That's what I've been feeling— the crystals call?" Luna asks, pressing a hand to her stomach when the feeling of an invisible rope pulling on her had her stomach knotting.

"Yes, and you will need to let those feelings guide you. But be wary of the blood crystal's pull. It will test your weakness and tempt you with your wildest dreams. You must trust yourself to tell the difference between good and evil."

Luna felt a flicker of fear, but the call of the crystals resonated deep within her. It was a feeling she couldn't ignore— a pull that demanded her attention. Luna swallows the lump in her throat and takes a deep breath before releasing it. Luna felt that the journey would be harrowing and wrought with challenges. And her wolf howled and clawed at its cage, ready to run, fight, and, Gods willing, win.

With Hunter by her side, Luna swallowed her apprehension. She took a deep breath and steadied her gaze on Sapphire. "When do we leave?"

Sapphire's wide smile conveyed unwavering confidence. "Let's arm you first, Princess," she replied, setting them on the path to an adventure that would test their limits, challenge their courage, and ultimately determine the fate of their world.

☾

Luna stood in the armory, her eyes wide with awe as she took in the vast array of weapons that adorned the walls. Swords, battle axes, clubs, and daggers of all shapes and sizes filled the room, each one holding a story untold. Luna's heart swelled with excitement, but a flicker of doubt crept into her mind.

"I haven't trained with most of these weapons," she confessed, her voice tinged with uncertainty. "How can I fight when I don't know how to use them?"

Her guards chuckled, their laughter echoing through the armory. Sapphire, her trusted advisor and mentor, smiled down at her.

"Fear not, Princess," Sapphire reassured her. "There is one weapon here meant for you and only you."

Curiosity piqued, Luna watched as Sapphire approached a long, ornate box. As the lid lifted, beams of ethereal light danced from within, captivating Luna's attention. She took a step forward, her eyes fixed on the mysterious contents of the box. Her breath caught in her throat when she laid her eyes upon the object within.

It was a sword, a thing of pure beauty. Its hilt gleamed with silver, and its blade shone like moonlight. The insignia on the pommel matched the necklace Luna wore, and a sense of familiarity washed over her.

Luna's voice trembled with a mix of awe and realization. "This...this was my mother's sword. Is that why I am the only one who can touch it?"

Sapphire nodded, her eyes filled with pride. "Your mother was a formidable warrior. She would train tirelessly, surpassing even the most skilled guards. This sword, *Kardiá* (heart), symbolized her power and legacy."

Luna's mind whirled with emotions while one question tapped at her lips. "It's massive. How am I supposed to hide this from the humans on my journey among humans?"

Sapphire grinned smugly. "You will see, Princess. But you must claim *Kardiá* first."

Though excitement coursed through her veins, Luna's hands shook nervously as she reached out to grasp the sword. As her fingers wrapped around the hilt, a surge of energy shot through her, and the armory melted away.

In its place stood a vast training ground surrounded by towering stone walls. Luna's heart quickened as she heard the clash of metal and the grunts of combatants.

"Come now, little princess, you can do better than that," a man's teasing voice echoes around the open room. *"Have I not trained you well enough?"* He chuckles.

"You have taught me just fine, Z. That is the problem, though, isn't it?" The woman grunted, and the man's back came into view as his arm swung to block her sword from knicking his face. He was tall with broad shoulders, midnight black hair that reached just to his collar, and obsidian eyes.

"How is that, little princess?" the man asked and parried out of the way of the woman's sword, sharp point. The woman lunged, her white blonde hair cascading down her chest and back, her icy blue eyes focused on the man, and her ruby lips lifted in a smirk as she sliced the sleeve of the man's shirt. The man halted, looked down at his torn sleeve, then back to the woman with a look of something that tickled Luna's belly and warmed her chest.

"You are the one who taught me, Z, and it is clear that you taught me only enough to defeat anyone who is not you." She stepped toward the man and placed the tip of her sword under his chin. The man tilted his head back with a grin and dropped his sword to the ground. The loud clang of metal against stone sent chills along Luna's skin.

"Perhaps you are right," the man, Z, said and brought his hand to the woman's hand on the grip of her sword. *"Perhaps I do not wish to fight you, little princess. Instead, what I desire is to kiss you."*

The woman smirked and came closer to Z, looking up at him with devotion. "You are bold, soldier. To speak to me in such a way could be seen as treasonous," she warned, but her words held no threat.

The man slowly lowered their hands, and the sword pummel appeared. "Kardiá," *Luna gasped as the realization set in. She knew who the couple was.*

Her mother and father.

"Then I will die a happy man with your kiss on my lips," the man said before his lips descended and...

The room swirls, the stone walls fade, and the armory shifts back into focus.

"Luna, are you alright?" Hunter asked, his voice laced with worry.

Luna blinked away the remnants of the vision, a bittersweet smile gracing her lips. "I saw them, Hunter. My parents... They were so in love." Her voice trembled with sadness and wonder.

Sapphire's voice broke through her reverie, reminding her of her purpose. "They were, very much, and it is tragic how it ended, but you cannot let it cloud your duty, Luna. Now, press your thumb to the insignia on the pommel."

Luna's brows furrowed in confusion, but she followed Sapphire's instructions. As her thumb made contact, the blade of *Kardiá* emitted a mechanical click, and it began to transform. The blade separated into four parts and then folded in on itself, becoming significantly smaller.

Marius, another guard, couldn't contain his excitement. "Whoa, that's seriously cool!"

Sapphire beamed with pride. "The mystics have endowed *Kardiá* with incredible abilities. Now, with a simple touch, you can wield it in its full glory or conceal it when necessary."

Luna pressed her thumb to the insignia once more, and the blade expanded back to its original length, towering above her head. A sense of empowerment surged through her.

"Yes, they can," Luna said, a determined glint in her eyes. "With *Kardiá* in hand, I am ready to face whatever challenges lie ahead. My parents' legacy lives on within me."

5

Luna took a deep breath and hummed a relaxing breath on the exhale. She knew she and her guards were in for a harrowing journey, and Luna would be lying if she said she wasn't scared. But with the fear came a thrill of excitement. It pulsed through her veins and made her wolf circle and leap with the need to hunt.

With her guards at her back and a map and compass enchanted by the mystics, Luna was ready to find the crystals and end the Dark Wolf's threat to this world.

The night was chilly as they started, and the moon luminous from above guided their path until they reached the thick forest.

Luna clutched the enchanted map and compass close to her chest, its magical properties pulsing with energy. It was a gift from the mystics, bestowed upon her to aid in her quest to find the mystical crystals that would vanquish the Dark Wolf.

"I beg you, Luna, stay in the middle of the pack," Aria spoke behind Luna.

Luna smiled to herself. Aria was only a couple months older than Luna, but she fretted over her like a mother hen. "And I beg you, Ari, let's not have the same conversation repeatedly. You four have taught me well, and I want to be the leader who fights beside her people, not one who stands on the sidelines watching her pack fight for her."

Aria let out a heavy sigh and grumbled, "Fine."

Her loyal guards stood at her back, their eyes sharp and senses heightened, but Luna's determination burned bright, and she refused to be a mere observer in her own destiny.

As the night grew colder, the moon guided their path, its luminescence dancing atop the dingy asphalt.

"Stay close, Luna," Aria pleaded, her voice tinged with concern. But Luna smiled, her confidence radiating like a beacon in the darkness.

"Take it easy, my friend," she reassured. "I'm going to fight beside you, shoulder to shoulder, not cowering on the sidelines."

They continued to walk through the streets, and Luna again wished they could take some type of public transportation to the edge of town until they reached the forest, where they would transform and unleash the power of their primal instincts. Luna felt the wolf stir within her, its hunger for the hunt awakening.

Still, the council had deemed it necessary for Luna and her comrades to undertake this perilous mission on foot because their journey was not just about retrieving the crystals. It was a battle to protect the very essence of humankind, to thwart the encroaching darkness that threatened to consume their world. They needed to be vigilant and ready to face any danger head-on.

Suddenly, a terrified cry pierced the night. "Mommy!" Luna's ears pricked up, and her instincts took over. Across the busy street stood a young girl, alone and frightened. Luna's heart quickened as she watched the child step into the path of an oncoming delivery van, oblivious to the dangers.

A tingle shot up Luna's spine, and her heart raced as her wolf bared its teeth. Without hesitation, Luna leaped into action. Her limbs moved with grace and speed. She reached the girl just as the van swerved, the impact grazing her shoulder and sending her crashing to the ground. Pain shot through her body, but her hold on the little girl remained tight as Luna held the child close, shielding her from harm as they rolled to safety.

Luna's wolf whimpered in pain as her body came to a thudding halt against the curb to the sounds of shocked murmurs. Her shoulder pulsed with pain, and her skin burned with road rash. The crowd's murmurs mingled with Luna's low groan of pain. But there was no time to dwell on her injuries or the attention they had attracted.

"Maddie!" Luna released the little girl from the safety of her arms at the girl's mother's relieved cry.

"Mommy!" the little girl shouts back and sprints from Luna's arms unharmed.

"Oh, thank God," the woman exclaimed. "Maddie, what were you thinking? Don't you ever do that again!"

"I'm sorry, Mommy!" the little girl sniffles, and the woman soothes her in a tight hug.

As Luna rose to her feet, her guards were steady and supportive. She knew her body was already healing itself, but she still winced as she took a step away from the crowd of people. The pack needed to leave before they attracted any more attention.

"Thank you so much," the woman said to Luna's back.

Luna nodded, acknowledging her words with a humble smile, before turning her gaze towards the street where the van had nearly run them down, but it had disappeared as if swallowed by the night, leaving Luna with a lingering sense of unease. She couldn't help but think the poison of the Dark Wolf was to blame.

The pack pressed forward, determination etched on their faces. Luna's shoulder pulsed with pain, her skin still raw from the impact. Yet, her spirit burned brighter than ever, fueled by the knowledge that their mission was greater than any obstacle they faced.

6

The scrapes and road burn had healed by the time the group reached the other side of the street, much to the surprise of Luna's soldiers. The power of healing within Luna was an extraordinary gift that she had only recently discovered. As they continued their journey, Luna's mind was filled with thoughts of the battles that lay ahead.

Hunter, one of Luna's most loyal guards, voiced his concern. "That could have been a disaster, Luna. We can't afford to reveal our true nature to humans. They fear what they don't understand."

Luna turned to Hunter, her eyes filled with determination. "I know the risks, Hunter. But when it comes down to it, I will always choose to protect human lives. I am here to help humankind and won't let fear hold me back."

Hunter's words were clipped, harboring a hint of resentment. "I apologize, your majesty. I just worry about your safety and the safety of the pack. We can't reveal what we are. Humans become angry, even violent when they come across things they don't understand. We could be lynched or taken to be studied and used for research. You have to—"

"Enough." Luna scolded. "I've heard all of this before. It's been drilled into my head for the past five years. But when it comes down to deciding to save a human life or walk by while one is in harm's way, I will make that decision for myself, and you will not question me, soldier." Luna hated speaking to her loyal guard and friend in such a way, but she knew if she didn't make things clear to Hunter now, he would question every move she made, and she didn't need him filling her head with doubt.

Luna sighed, understanding Hunter's concerns. She placed a hand on his shoulder, reassuring him. "I appreciate your concern, Hunter. But I need you to trust in me. I have the pack's well-being in mind, but I won't let fear dictate my actions."

Hunter nodded, his face filled with a mixture of respect and understanding. Luna's words had struck a chord within him, reminding him of their shared purpose. With renewed determination, the group continued their journey.

As they walked, the streets filled with vibrant party-goers, their laughter and joyous hoots filling the air. Luna's gaze wandered, her heart filled with a bittersweet longing. Despite her extraordinary abilities as a wolf, a part of Luna yearned for a normal life. She longed to be an ordinary girl, experiencing the simple joys of teenagehood like going to school, going to the movies with friends, crushing on a boy— though she had to admit she accomplished the latter. But she knew that her destiny lay elsewhere, and she had accepted it.

Galic, always the practical one, interrupted Luna's thoughts with a reminder. "We need to find shelter and rest soon. You've begun to heal but still need to regain your full strength."

Luna nodded, acknowledging Galic's concerns. She scanned the area, her eyes landing on a pizzeria with a checkered awning and the mouthwatering scent of food wafting from within. A sense of familiarity drew her towards the cozy establishment. Something that felt like coming home on a cold day to sit in front of the fire. Like familiarity.

Entering the pizzeria, Luna was greeted by the sounds of a woman passionately speaking in Italian to a man who appeared to be the chef. The feeling grew the longer Luna stood there. As the couple's eyes locked on Luna, a spark of recognition flickered in their gazes.

"Do I know you?" Luna asked, her voice filled with curiosity. "Something about this place feels familiar."

The woman stammered, her eyes welling with tears. "Your Majesty," she uttered, bowing before Luna, swatting her hand against the man's barrel-like chest. The man snapped out of his shocked state and followed suit, his expression shining with surprise and reverence.

Luna's eyes widened in astonishment. "How do you know who I am?"

The woman's voice trembled with emotion as she spoke. "Have you received your mother's sword?"

Now, it was Luna who stumbled back in surprise. "Yes, I have. Why?"

The woman smiled sweetly, unshed tears twinkling in her eyes. "Then that is why you felt the pull. We were friends and confidants of your mother. You felt the pull towards this place because you now have her memories, her familiarities."

Luna's heart raced as she realized the significance of their words. The pizzeria that had drawn her in held secrets intimately connected to her mother. Standing face to face with these strangers who claimed to have known her, Luna couldn't help but be overcome with curiosity and apprehension.

With her worn hands and kind eyes, the woman spoke with a softness that belied the weight of her words. "Your mother, she was a remarkable woman. A warrior with a heart of gold, just like you." Luna's mind raced with thoughts and questions.

But Galic stepped forward, his gaze fixed on the woman. "If what you say is true, Luna has inherited more than just her mother's sword. She carries a legacy, a burden even, that she may not fully understand."

The woman nodded knowingly, her eyes welling up with tears. "Your mother fought bravely against the forces of darkness alongside her companions in many battles. That is until…" The women winced.

Though Luna knew the story of her mother's demise and that Luna was the chosen one, she hadn't realized the depth of her connection with her mother. Luna's eyes widened in disbelief. She had her mother's memories to guide her. Knowing that her destiny was intricately tied to a battle against darkness that killed her mother? Her mother died in childbirth, but had the darkness begun even before that night? She felt a surge of conflicting emotions — fear and anger— and a sense of duty to carry on her mother's legacy.

The man, who had remained silent until now, stepped forward. His presence commanded attention, his broad frame and weathered face a testament to a lifetime of battles fought. "Luna, my name is Dimitri. I was your mother's closest ally and guardian. We were entrusted with protecting the world from the forces of darkness. And now, it is your turn to take up that mantle."

Luna felt a rush of emotions wash over her. Not long ago, she was just an ordinary girl. How could she possibly be expected to fight against the dark forces that threatened to engulf the world? But as she looked into Dimitri's eyes, she saw a flicker of hope and determination that resonated deep within her.

With a newfound sense of purpose, Luna squared her shoulders and nodded. "I may not know much about my mother's past, but I'm willing to learn. I'm willing to fight. For her, for the world."

The pizzeria seemed to hum with otherworldly energy as if the spirits of the fallen warriors were watching, lending their support to Luna's resolve.

"Please sit. You must be starving." The woman gestured to a table with the same checkered material as the awning outside and a low flickering candle in a glass jar.

As Luna and her companions sat, she couldn't help but feel a mixture of trepidation and excitement. The path ahead was uncertain, but she was no longer alone.

With her mother's memories and familiarities pulsing through her veins, Luna took another step towards embracing her destiny as a warrior of her people, ready to face the forces that awaited her.

7

After a delicious meal of two meat-lovers pizzas, salad, and chocolate cannoli, Luna was stuffed and ready to put this night to rest.

"Please, you must stay with us. We have a spare room. There is only one bed, but the carpet is thick. It should be comfortable enough with your bed packs," Dimitri offered.

"Oh, no, we couldn't impose on you like that," Luna replied out of courtesy when what she really wanted to do was collapse on the spot.

Dimitri shooed her words away with a flourish of his hand. "It would be an honor to host you for the evening, Your Majesty."

"Then it's settled," Hunter speaks. "We will sleep here tonight and start back up in the morning." Luna gazed at the handsome boy in appreciation. She didn't mind that he made the final decision because she knew it came from a place of respect and concern. Her wounds stopped healing the more Luna became fatigued, and Hunter was willing to step up and take control for the sake of her health.

"Wonderful," Dimitri cheered and gestured for them to follow him, where he guided them to a set of stairs in the back of the restaurant. The door to their temporary sanctuary revealed itself at the end of the corridor, an imposing slab of solid steel adorned with intricate engravings that spoke of a forgotten time. Dimitri inserted a key into the lock, turning it with a soft click, and the door swung open to reveal a spacious yet cozy room.

As Luna and her companions entered the small room they would occupy for the night, their weariness began to weigh on them like invisible chains. The scent of aged wood and forgotten memories filled the air.

Moonlight filtered through the curtains, casting a gentle glow that danced upon the antique furniture. A large, ornate bed dominated the room, its mahogany frame exuding a sense of grandeur. The thick carpet, seemingly untouched by time, beckoned tired feet to sink into its plush embrace.

Decorating the walls were tapestries depicting scenes from long-lost lands and mythical creatures. Luna found herself captivated by a tapestry depicting a majestic winged horse soaring through a midnight sky, its silver mane shimmering as if touched by starlight. It was as though the room itself held secrets and dreams that had been carefully woven into the fabric of its being.

As Luna explored further, she discovered a small writing desk tucked away in a corner. It was adorned with quills, inkwells, and parchment. The desk seemed to invite creativity and the pursuit of knowledge, providing a sanctuary for the wandering mind to find solace and inspiration.

As Dimitri bid them goodnight and closed the door, Luna felt a sense of calm wash over her. With its tapestries and antique furniture, the room felt like a haven from the storm that brewed outside. It was as if the very essence of her mother weaved through the air, promising intrigue and adventure while offering respite and peace.

At that moment, Luna realized that this room was more than just a resting place. It was a sanctuary where the boundary between the ordinary and the extraordinary blurred, and the whispers of the past danced upon the air. She knew that within its walls, her body would heal, and her journey would continue.

And so, Luna and the others settled into the room, finding comfort in its embrace. They drifted into a peaceful slumber, their dreams intertwining with the secrets whispered by the room itself. As the night unfolded, memories stirred in her dreams, awaiting their awakening and the adventures ahead.

As the group gathered their belongings, the morning sun shone through the gap in the heavy curtains. The air was crisp and filled with anticipation.

Just as the first rays of sunlight painted the sky in hues of pink and orange, a soft knock echoed through the room. Hunter, ever vigilant, quickly grabbed his longsword and moved towards the door. "Who is it?" he called out, his voice laced with caution.

"It is I, Dimitri," a warm voice responded from the other side. Hunter cautiously opened the door, just enough to confirm the visitor's identity. Dimitri stood there, a kind smile on his face and a small bundle of pastries wrapped in wax paper in his hands.

Dimitri entered the room with a gracious nod of thanks, the aroma of freshly baked pastries wafting through the air. He placed them gently on the bed, their golden, flaky crusts tempting the senses. "For your morning journey," he said, his voice filled with genuine kindness before he returned to the hallway and reappeared with four large thermoses of what promised to be rich, aromatic espresso. The scent filled the room, invigorating and energizing. "You are young but never too young for real Italian espresso," he proclaimed proudly. "None of that wretched vacuum-sealed stuff for Your Majesty."

Luna's face lit up with gratitude as she accepted the offered thermos, her gaze meeting Dimitri's. "Thank you, Dimitri," she said sincerely. "Your generosity knows no bounds. We are truly fortunate to have crossed paths with someone as kind-hearted as you."

Dimitri bowed deeply, his eyes shining with humility. "It has been my pleasure to assist you," he replied. "May you find strength and courage on your journey, and may the heavens shine upon you always."

With a final nod of gratitude, the group carefully packed the pastries and thermoses into their bags, recognizing the preciousness of Dimitri's gift. The weight of anticipation hung in the air, mingling with the rich aroma of espresso.

As they prepared to leave, a sudden commotion filled the streets outside. The sharp, shrill sound of smoke detectors pierced the stillness, accompanied by frightened shouts from the pedestrians below. Luna's sensitive ears perked up, and her wolf stirred within her.

Luna's companions glanced at each other, their eyes reflecting concern and readiness. They knew they would face countless challenges together, and this unexpected disturbance only fueled their determination.

The group rushed towards the window, their hearts pounding in their chests. Outside, smoke billowed from the pizzeria, its acrid scent filling the air. Panic spread like wildfire through the crowd, but Luna's wolf rose amidst the chaos, ready to protect and guide them through the impending danger.

"Stay close," Luna's voice rang out, her tone steady and unwavering. "We will face whatever challenges come our way, for we are bound by a shared purpose and hearts filled with courage." Luna had no idea where those words came from but didn't have time to ponder their origin.

The group set off towards the source of the disturbance, their footsteps mingling with the crowd's cries and the blaring alarms.

"I am here amore mia." Luna heard Dimitri yelling through a closed door while his wife screamed for help. When they reached the bottom of the stairs, Luna ordered the others to get Dimitri out while she and Hunter rescued the woman. "No! I will not leave her," Dimitri cried, but he was no match for the youthful strength of the others as they dragged him for the burning building.

The air was thick with smoke, choking Luna as she pushed through the burning wreckage. The crackling flames clawed at the ceiling, hungrily devouring everything in their path. Luna's heart raced in her chest, matching the urgency of her mission. She had to find Dimitri's wife trapped somewhere within the flaming inferno.

As Luna and Hunter reached the door leading to the room where Dimitri's wife was trapped, a wave of despair washed over them. The heat had melted the metal, sealing the door shut as if it were part of the structure itself.

"It's melted shut, but that's impossible," Hunter voiced Luna's thoughts on a ragged cough.

Luna's mind raced, desperately searching for a solution. She closed her eyes, tapping into the depths of her power, calling upon the spirits of her ancestors for guidance.

A surge of energy coursed through her veins, and Luna's eyes snapped open, illuminating the darkness around her with a piercing blue light. Her transformation began, her body shifting, morphing into a creature of the night. Her teeth elongated into sharp fangs, and her nails grew into razor-sharp claws. Luna drew her mother's sword, a weapon steeped in ancient magic, and held it aloft, channeling her mother's strength.

She brought the gleaming steel to her forehead and spoke. "Help me, Mother. Let my strike be strong and true." Instantly, the sword whirled and clinked into place.

With a thunderous strike, Luna brought the sword down upon the welded edge of the door. The metal shrieked and groaned, giving way beneath the force of her blow. Hunter, his eyes filled with awe, pulled the door open, revealing Dimitri's wife lying unconscious in the room.

But their escape was barred by a massive flaming beam, collapsing in front of the front door. Luna's mind raced once more, searching for an alternative exit. Hunter's voice broke through the chaos, directing their attention to the back door. They rushed towards it, hearts pounding, only to find their path again obstructed.

Desperation washed over them, their options dwindling. Luna and Hunter locked eyes, a silent understanding passing between them. They had no choice but to resort to their primal nature and fully transform into the creatures they were.

Shaking the woman in his arms, Hunter spoke. "Hey. Wake up." The woman stirred, and her eyes fluttered open slightly. "We need to change. When we do, you're going to have to get on my back and hang on," he explained to the woman, who nodded weakly.

Hunter placed her on the floor, and then, in unison, Luna and Hunter shed their human forms, their bodies reshaping into majestic wolves. Luna's coat became pure white with a long, red strip of human hair on her head. Hunter transformed into a massive brown wolf, his eyes radiating a vibrant green glow.

The woman stumbled onto Hunter's back, where she collapsed but kept a tight grip on his fur. With their instincts as guides, Luna and Hunter prepared to make their daring escape through the flames. They communicated effortlessly, a bond forged by shared experiences and unwavering trust. Counting silently to three, Hunter's powerful hind legs propelled them forward, launching them through the fiery barrier.

Glass shattered around them as they burst through the back entrance, landing on solid ground outside. The air, though still tainted with smoke, was a relief compared to the suffocating heat of the burning building. Luna and Hunter resumed their human forms, the weight of their actions bearing heavily upon their weary bodies.

Hunter picked the woman up again. They jogged around the building where firefighters were already working hard to extinguish the fire. Dimitri's anguished howl pierced the air as he spotted his wife cradled in Hunter's arms.

Turning her gaze back to the smoldering ruins, Luna knew that the darkness responsible for this devastation was growing stronger, its grip tightening on the world.

With resolve burning bright within her, she vowed to protect humanity by seeking out the crystals and restoring the balance. The darkness may provoke and threaten, but Luna would not succumb to the allure of revenge. She would face the challenges ahead with unwavering courage, her wolf snarling defiantly in the face of darkness.

Dear reader,

Apologies for the delay in sharing Luna's full story. In the midst of school, family, and endless adventures, time slipped away. But fear not, the next installment of her story will be unveiled soon, taking you to breathtaking landscapes and introducing you to extraordinary characters.

As you eagerly await the continuation, remember to follow me on Instagram for sneak peeks, behind-the-scenes insights, and more thrilling updates.

Adventure awaits, my dear reader. Prepare to be swept away.

Yours in imagination,
Camilla Wolfe
http://www.instagram.com/author_camillawolfe

JOURNEY OF THE WOLF

Made in the USA
Coppell, TX
17 November 2023

24260053R00031